Chicken Licken

by Jackie Walter and Emma Latham

FRANKLIN WATTS
LONDON • SYDNEY

One sunny day, Chicken Licken went
for a walk in the woods.
As he walked along, an acorn fell
on his head.
"Oh, no!" cried Chicken Licken.
"The sky is falling. I must go
to the palace to tell the king!"

So off he went.

On the way, he met Henny Penny.

"Where are you going?"
asked Henny Penny.

"The sky is falling!" cried Chicken Licken.

"I'm going to the palace to tell the king."

"I'll come with you," said Henny Penny.

So off they went.

On the way, they met Cocky Locky.

"Where are you going?"

asked Cocky Locky.

"The sky is falling!" cried Chicken Licken.

6

"We're going to the palace to tell
the king," said Henny Penny.
"I'll come with you," said Cocky Locky.

So off they went.

On the way, they met Ducky Lucky.

"Where are you going?"

asked Ducky Lucky.

"The sky is falling!" cried Chicken Licken.

"We're going to the palace to tell
the king," said Henny Penny.
"We must be quick!" said Cocky Locky.
"I'll come with you," said Ducky Lucky.

So off they went.

On the way, they met Goosey Loosey.

"Where are you going?"
asked Goosey Loosey.

"The sky is falling!" cried Chicken Licken.

"We're going to the palace to tell
the king," said Henny Penny.
"We must be quick," said Cocky Locky.
"It may be too late!" cried Ducky Lucky.
"I'll come with you," said Goosey Loose

1

So off they went.

On the way, they met Turkey Lurkey.

"Where are you going?"
asked Turkey Lurkey.

"The sky is falling!" cried Chicken Licken.

"We're going to the palace to tell
the king," said Henny Penny.

"We must be quick," said Cocky Locky.

"It may be too late!" cried Ducky Lucky.

"We might die!" cried Goosey Loosey.

"I'll come with you," said Turkey Lurkey.

So off they went.

On the way, they met Foxy Loxy.

And Foxy Loxy was hungry.

"Hello there," said Foxy Loxy.

"Where are you going?"

"The sky is falling!" cried Chicken Licken.
"We're going to the palace to tell
the king!"

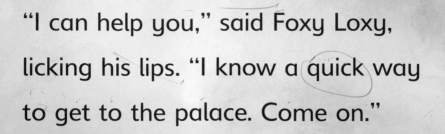

"I can help you," said Foxy Loxy,
licking his lips. "I know a quick way
to get to the palace. Come on."

16

Chicken Licken, Henny Penny,
Cocky Locky, Ducky Lucky,
Goosey Loosey and Turkey Lurkey
went into Foxy Loxy's den ...

... and they were never seen again.

Story order

Look at these 5 pictures and captions.
Put the pictures in the right order
to retell the story.

1

Foxy Loxy said he knew a quick
way to the palace.

2

Chicken Licken told Goosey Loosey
about the sky falling in.

3

An acorn fell on Chicken Licken.

4

The birds were never seen again.

5

Chicken Licken ran to tell the king.

Guide for Independent Reading

This series is designed to provide an opportunity for your child to read on their own. These notes are written for you to help your child choose a book and to read it independently.

In school, your child's teacher will often be using reading books which have been banded to support the process of learning to read. Use the book band colour your child is reading in school to help you make a good choice. *Chicken Licken* is a good choice for children reading at Turquoise Band in their classroom to read independently.

The aim of independent reading is to read this book with ease, so that your child enjoys the story and relates it to their own experiences.

About the book

When an acorn drops on Chicken Licken, he is sure the sky is falling. He sets off to the palace to tell the king, bringing many of his friends along, too. Then they all get tricked by the cunning Foxy Loxy.

Before reading

Help your child to learn how to make good choices by asking: "Why did you choose this book? Why do you think you will enjoy it?" Look at the cover together and ask: "What do you think the story will be about?" Ask your child to think of what they already know about the story context. Then ask your child to read the title aloud.

Ask: "What do you think has happened to Chicken Licken?" Remind your child that they can sound out a word in syllable chunks if they get stuck.

Decide together whether your child will read the story independently or read it aloud to you.

During reading
Remind your child of what they know and what they can do independently. If reading aloud, support your child if they hesitate or ask for help by telling the word. If reading to themselves, remind your child that they can come and ask for your help if stuck.

After reading
Support comprehension by asking your child to tell you about the story. Use the story order puzzle to encourage your child to retell the story in the right sequence, in their own words. The correct sequence can be found on the next page.

Help your child think about the messages in the book that go beyond the story and ask: "Why do you think everyone believes Chicken Licken? How is Foxy Loxy able to trick the birds into following him?" Give your child a chance to respond to the story: "Did you have a favourite part? Do you think it is important to ask questions about things before you believe them?"

Extending learning
Help your child understand the story structure by using the same sentence patterning and adding different elements. "Let's make up a new story about Chicken Licken. What might happen to him this time? How could the story end differently?"

In the classroom, your child's teacher may be teaching use of punctuation marks. Ask your child to identify some question marks and exclamation marks in the story and then ask them to practise reading each of the whole sentences with appropriate expression.

Franklin Watts
First published in Great Britain in 2021
by The Watts Publishing Group

Copyright © The Watts Publishing Group 2021

Series Editors: Jackie Hamley and Melanie Palmer
Series Advisors: Dr Sue Bodman and Glen Franklin
Series Designers: Peter Scoulding and Cathryn Gilbert

A CIP catalogue record for this book is
available from the British Library.

ISBN 978 1 4451 7700 7 (hbk)
ISBN 978 1 4451 7701 4 (pbk)
ISBN 978 1 4451 7699 4 (library ebook)
ISBN 978 1 4451 8176 9 (ebook)

Printed in China

Franklin Watts
An imprint of
Hachette Children's Group
Part of The Watts Publishing Group
Carmelite House
50 Victoria Embankment
London EC4Y 0DZ

An Hachette UK Company
www.hachette.co.uk

www.franklinwatts.co.uk

Answer to Story order: 3, 5, 2, 1, 4